SHANE COCHRAN

Written by Ian Boyd
3-D Imaging by Jim Bostwick
Design by A. Kerr

Thanks to the following zoos, photographers, and companies
who generously provided photos for *Outrageous 3-D Big Bugs:*

Brookfield Zoo/Chicago Zoological Society, 3300 Golf, Brookfield, Illinois 60513
Lubber grasshopper, page 19 (photographer: Jim Schulz)
Special thanks to Nancy Pajeau for her help in locating images for this book.

Corel Corporation
Praying mantis, page 5 and back cover; *Cicada,* page 7; *Shield bug,* page 9; *Giant water bug,* page 11;
Long-horned beetle, page 13 and cover; *Millipede,* page 17; *Rhinoceros beetle,* page 23

Entomological Society of America/Ries Memorial Slide Collection, 9301 Annapolis Road, Lanham, Maryland 20706
Assassin bug, page 15; *Sphinx moth,* page 21
Special thanks to Denise McCall for her help in locating images for this book.

Printed in the United States of America. ISBN 0-8167-4354-1

10 9 8 7 6 5 4 3 2 1

Contents

Introduction

Beware of the Big Bug!

Little bugs are everywhere. No matter where you look—in the grass, on a sidewalk, or even inside your house—you can find these small, six-legged creatures. But big bugs are another story. You probably won't ever journey beneath a pond's surface to see the massive pincer-claws of a 6-inch (15-cm) giant water bug. And you would have a hard time finding a 5-inch (12.5-cm) praying mantis, since they are so well hidden in the wild. But with *Outrageous 3-D Big Bugs*, you can get close to these big bugs and more.

In this book, you'll see ten big, outrageous bugs in stunning, page-popping 3-D. And the special viewer that comes with the book brings each immense insect to life. Not only will you see a praying mantis holding out its spiny arms, you'll be able to see each spine in fabulous detail. You'll also see a giant lubber grasshopper coming toward you through a maze of weeds and branches and get a "bird's-eye" view of a beautiful sphinx moth perched on a flower.

So sit back, grab your 3-D viewer, and watch the amazing world of big bugs come to life. Take your time looking at each picture— you may be surprised at what you'll find in 3-D!

Praying Mantis

Armed to Eat

The praying mantis in this photograph wants to give you a big hug—that is, if you're another praying mantis! People who study insects think a female praying mantis sometimes extends her front legs when a male approaches, as if to say, "Don't worry, you're welcome here." But if the legs are down, the female may be feeling hungry. Mantises will eat each other, so the male had better stay away if he doesn't want to turn into a meal!

Perhaps this 5-inch (12.5-cm) *carnivore*, or meat-eater, should also be called a "preying" mantis, because it loves to prey on beetles, caterpillars, crickets, and grasshoppers. Some mantids will sit still without eating for weeks, waiting for an unsuspecting bug to crawl near. When one does, the lightning-quick mantis snatches it up for a savory snack.

A mantis's grayish-green or grayish-brown skin color blends in with surrounding grass and trees, making it nearly invisible. Not only does this special coloring help the mantis to surprise prey, it also keeps the bug from being spotted and eaten by hungry birds.

The praying mantis in this picture has its front legs open, but these creatures are named for the way they usually hold their legs—together in front of their bodies, as if praying.

5

Cicada

Natural Buzzers

Step outside on a summer evening, and you will probably hear the buzz of a cicada (suh-KAY-duh). Then again, you may not even have to open the door, because cicadas are the loudest insects in the world. The high-pitched song of these bugs can travel nearly a quarter of a mile (402 m)—a length of more than three and a half football fields! But only male cicadas have sound-producing organs. Females can't make a sound.

There are two groups of cicadas in North America: dog-day cicadas and periodical cicadas. Most cicadas are between 1 and 2 inches (2.5 and 5 cm) long, but cicadas more than 4 inches (10 cm) long have been found in the tropical jungles of Malaysia in Southeast Asia.

No matter where they live, cicadas spend most of their lives underground as wormlike *nymphs*, emerging only when they are full-grown. A dog-day cicada takes four years to emerge. A periodical cicada waits longer—either thirteen or seventeen years! Once a cicada crawls out of the soil, it begins looking for a mate. But it shouldn't waste any time, because cicadas live just a few weeks after they emerge from their underground nests.

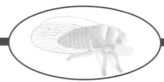

Like many other hard-shelled insects, cicadas must *molt*, or shed their skins, before becoming adults. The cicada in this picture is a young adult, so its hollow skin-shell is still clinging to a tree somewhere!

7

Shield Bug

Call Me "Stink Bug"

If you ever come across a shield bug in the wild, keep walking. Shield bugs can produce a strong-smelling chemical on demand, and they won't hesitate to use it on you! As if that isn't bad enough, one type of giant shield bug in Australia squirts a liquid that can cause temporary blindness. These bugs are pests, not pets!

Despite their built-in defenses, shield bugs don't look as if they would pose much of a threat. Most shield bugs are small (though some, like the one in the picture to the right, are more than 1½ inches [3.8 cm] long). And with their red, green, and orange shells, shield bugs boast some of the most beautiful colors in the insect world. But to birds and other predators, a shield bug might as well be wearing a "Do Not Disturb" sign, because flashy colors in nature usually mean danger.

Shield bugs produce more than just dangerous chemicals. They also produce special sounds to attract mates by rubbing parts of their legs on their abdomens in much the same way a violinist draws a bow across the violin strings.

It's easy to see where this bug gets its name. A large, shield-shaped plate, or *scutellum* (skyoo-TELL-em), covers much of a shield bug's body. With only its legs and the tip of its head sticking out, the shield bug is safe from most predators.

Giant Water Bug

Don't Go in the Water!

Reaching up to 6 inches (15 cm) in length, giant water bugs lurk beneath the surfaces of many North American ponds and streams. A little oxygen goes a long way with these bugs, which can go hours or even days without resurfacing.

A giant water bug's size allows it to hunt for small water game such as salamanders, snakes, and fish. On a really good day, this big bug may even snag a bird. The water bug grabs its prey with two clawlike pincers, then injects an acidic digestive juice. The victim's insides turn to fluid, and the giant water bug slurps them all up for a nice meal. Now that's a real liquid diet!

Giant water bugs don't do all the eating. In some parts of the world, they are the ones being eaten. Many people in the Orient consider steamed, boiled, or roasted water bugs a delicacy. *"Giant water bugs! Get your hot, roasted giant water bugs!"*

Giant water bugs are nicknamed "toe biters." Some people have painfully learned why after dipping their feet in lakes and streams. *Ouch!* Don't worry, the water bug's bite can't turn *your* insides into slush.

11

Long-horned Beetle

Beetle-Mania!

Take a look at the photo on the right, and you'll know where these bugs got their name. Long-horned beetles' lengthy antennae, or "horns," may be several times longer than their bodies! These beetles don't qualify as big bugs just because of their amazing antennae, though. Some long-horned beetles living in the jungles of South America have bodies nearly 6 inches (15 cm) long!

The power of these insects is mind-boggling. Scientists put one long-horned beetle through a strength test and found that it could lift 850 times its own weight. That's like a 50-pound kid lifting a stack of more than twenty adult elephants!

Long-horned beetles are popular among insect collectors because of their bright, beautiful markings. Brilliant reds, yellows, and oranges are a few of the colors commonly found on these beetles. The black and yellow-orange pattern on one type of South American long-horned beetle is so striking that Amazon Indian men like to paint it on their shields.

This adult long-horned beetle is feeding on pollen, but as a grub (beetle larva) it preferred wood. The scraping sounds made by wood-munching beetle grubs are feared by log cabin owners, who know that these little critters can *truly* eat them out of house and home!

13

Assassin Bug

A Bug with an Attitude

If there was ever a bug suited to its name, it's the one you see here: an assassin bug. More than 1½ inches (3.8 cm) long, an assassin bug is larger than the average bug and far more ferocious. Assassin bugs eat mostly insects, but they occasionally attack creatures much larger than themselves, such as reptiles, birds, and mammals!

Once an assassin bug seizes an insect, it uses its curved mouth part to puncture the victim's body and suck out the insides. Grasshoppers and other insects try to avoid becoming another animal's dinner, but an assassin bug blends into tree bark and dead leaves, making it nearly impossible to spot. What's more, many assassin bugs *imitate*, or look like, some of the insects they prey upon. That's bad news for wasps and bees, two often-mimicked insects!

The news can be bad for humans, too. Not only do assassin bugs pack a painful bite, some also carry parasites and disease. In North America, there is even an assassin bug that bites people on the face and mouth. It's called a kissing bug!

This assassin bug is hiding out on a leaf, waiting for a six-legged meal to walk by. If bugs could talk, they would probably say that an assassin bug is the Tyrannosaurus of the insect world!

Millipede

Legs Galore

It's a good thing this millipede (MIHL-uh-peed) doesn't have to wear clothes. Imagine buying pants and shoes for all those legs! But that's nothing compared with millipedes found in the tropical rain forests of the world. Some giant millipedes there have 200 or more legs on their 12-inch (30-cm) bodies. Though the word "millipede" means "thousand-footed," even the largest millipedes have no more than 300 legs. Still, that's a lot of legs!

A millipede lurks in the soil beneath a rock or a rotten log until it gets hungry. Then it goes out in search of decaying plants to feed on. But away from home, this wormlike insect is an easy target for predators. So when confronted with danger, a millipede rolls itself up into a tight ball and plays dead. Some millipedes can also give off an awful-smelling odor to scare away would-be attackers, while others produce fluid that contains cyanide (SY-uh-nide), a highly poisonous chemical.

It seems funny that millipedes should have so many defenses. With all those legs, they should be able to outrun anything!

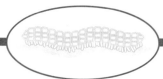

It would be almost impossible to count the legs on a moving millipede. But you may have better luck with the photo on the right. If you still can't count the legs, try counting the body segments. Each segment has two pairs of legs attached!

Lubber Grasshopper

"Clodhopper"

That six-legged creature peeking at you from its weedy perch is a lubber grasshopper. "Lubber" means big and clumsy, which is the perfect description for this creepy critter. With its heavy, 3-inch (7.5-cm) body and tiny wings, a lubber grasshopper won't set any flight records. Instead, it spends much of its time hopping about, stopping often to munch on leaves and grass.

Farmers consider lubber grasshoppers pests because they sometimes travel in large numbers, consuming anything they can find. Nothing is safe from their huge appetites. Alfalfa, corn, and cotton crops may be completely wiped out by a swarm of these marching critters. And when lubber grasshoppers cross the road to enter another field, motorists aren't safe either. Roads sometimes become as slick as ice when vehicles drive over masses of lubbers and squash their large bodies!

Grasshoppers are grouped according to the length of their antennae (an-TEHN-ee), or "horns." Lubber grasshoppers have small antennae and are called short-horned grasshoppers. But that's about the only thing that's small about these massive bugs!

This lubber grasshopper doesn't appear to be looking directly at you. But this bug's two large compound eyes each contain 5,000 individual lenses, allowing it to see everything around it—including you!

Sphinx Moth

Mighty Moth!

This sphinx (sfinks) moth is a lot like another winged creature, the hummingbird. A sphinx moth flies with the speed and grace of a hummingbird, flapping its wings so rapidly that it can hover in front of a flower. And some sphinx moths fly during the day instead of at night, when most moths are active. So it should come as no surprise to find that this marvelous moth is sometimes called a "hummingbird moth."

The adult sphinx moth has a powerful, streamlined body with a wingspan of more than 3½ inches (8.8 cm). But perhaps the most amazing part of a sphinx moth is its *proboscis*, a nectar-sipping tube that it keeps curled up outside its mouth. Uncoiled, this tube can probe flowers 10 inches (25 cm) away—nearly triple the moth's wingspan!

Sphinx moths get their name from something special they do when they're caterpillars. When a sphinx moth caterpillar wants to rest, it lifts the front part of its body off the ground and bows its head. From the side it resembles an Egyptian sphinx!

This picture gives you a bird's-eye view of a sphinx moth sipping nectar from a flower. It's a good thing for this moth that you aren't really a bird, because you'd probably swoop down and have it for a meal. Birds (and bats) feast on moths!

21

Rhinoceros Beetle

Armored Insect

It's no wonder this bug is called a rhinoceros beetle. Just look at that massive, low-to-the ground body and those intimidating horns! Although a rhinoceros beetle is much smaller than the animal it is named after, at 2½ inches (6.3 cm) it is the largest beetle in North America. But rhinoceros beetles nearly twice that size have been found in the rain forests of Central and South America.

Rhinoceros beetles use their great size and strength to fight one another during mating season. A male beetle tries to lift his opponent with his curved horns, then slam the opponent to the ground. The champion beetle usually walks off with first prize: a female rhinoceros beetle. The losing beetle's pride may suffer a few bumps and bruises, but not his body. He quickly gets up and goes looking for another fight.

Rhinoceros beetles belong to the *scarab* family. These heavy-bodied beetles were symbols of eternal life to the ancient Egyptians. Scarabs have been found carved in jewelry and painted on tombs.

The rhinoceros beetle in this photograph has little to worry about. A thick shell and two strong wing covers protect it from birds and other predators. This creature is the ultimate "armored tank" of the beetle world!

Go "Buggy"!

Now that you've finished your tour through the world of big bugs, you can see why some people consider these creatures to be the weirdest animals in nature. What other animals have hundreds of legs, produce poisonous chemicals, and can lift 850 times their own body weight?

There are about a million kinds of bugs in the world, all with their own remarkable traits. You can learn about these insects on your own. A library is a great place to start. You can also visit a museum or a zoo to find out more about bugs. Some zoos even have special *entomological* exhibits (areas where insects are kept and displayed) that you can visit.

When it comes to bugs, one thing is certain: The more you get to know them, the more outrageous they become!